OHIO
DOMINICAN
UNIVERSITY™

SINCE 1911

The
Cannibals

The
Cannibals

Starring
* Tiffany Spratt *

as told to

Cynthia D. Grant

Roaring Brook Press
Brookfield, Connecticut

Published by Roaring Brook Press
A division of The Millbrook Press, Inc.
2 Old New Milford Road
Brookfield, Connecticut 06804

Library of Congress Cataloging-in-Publication Data
Grant, Cynthia D.
The Cannibals: starring Tiffany Spratt / as told to Cynthia D. Grant.—1st ed.
p. cm.
Summary: In her journal the relentlessly superficial Tiffany, head of the cheerleading group called
the Cannibals, describes the excitement and turmoil of her senior year in high school.
[1. High schools—Fiction. 2. Schools—Fiction. 3. Diaries—Fiction.]
I. Title
PZ7.G76672 Can 2002

[Fic]—dc21

2002005915

ISBN 0-7613-1642-6 (trade)
1 3 5 7 9 10 8 6 4 2

ISBN 0-7613-2759-2 (library binding)
1 3 5 7 9 10 8 6 4 2

Book design by Jaye Zimet
Set in Helvetica Thin

Printed in the United States of America
First edition

For Miss Jones,
even though I still think
this should count toward my final grade.
—T.S.

For Ruth Walker,
with gratitude, affection,
and admiration.
—C.D.G.

The Cannibals